The Deep Freeze

adapted by Cordelia Evans

based on the screenplay written by Mélanie Duval

illustrated by Art Mawhinney and Shane L. Johnson

Ready-to-Read

Simon Spotlight

New York   London   Toronto   Sydney   New Delhi

SIMON SPOTLIGHT
An imprint of Simon & Schuster Children's Publishing Division
1230 Avenue of the Americas, New York, New York 10020
First Simon Spotlight edition September 2014
For information about special discounts for bulk purchases, please contact Simon & Schuster Special Sales at
1-866-506-1949 or business@simonandschuster.com.
The Simon & Schuster Speakers Bureau can bring authors to your live event.
For more information or to book an event contact the Simon & Schuster Speakers Bureau at 1-866-248-3049 or
visit our website at www.simonspeakers.com.
Manufactured in the United States of America 0814 LAK
2 4 6 8 10 9 7 5 3 1
ISBN 978-1-4814-0046-6 (hc)
ISBN 978-1-4814-0045-9 (pbk)
ISBN 978-1-4814-0047-3 (eBook)

CONTENTS

Chapter 1: Bwrrrrrr!   5

Chapter 2: Rabbid Tuna   11

Chapter 3: Store Surfing   18

Chapter 4: A New Tactic   24

Chapter 5: The Last Straw   32

Chapter 6: The Big Thaw   38

CHAPTER 1:
BWRRRRRR!

"*Pffffffft!* Bwa ha ha ha ha! *Pffffffft!* Bwa ha ha ha ha!"

A Rabbid in a grocery store was having a very fun time by himself blowing into a straw. This was probably fun to the Rabbid because the sound that came out of the straw sounded a lot like a sound that could come out of his butt, and that made him laugh.

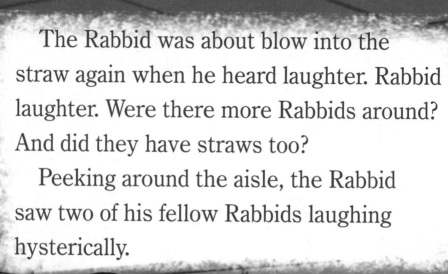

The Rabbid was about blow into the straw again when he heard laughter. Rabbid laughter. Were there more Rabbids around? And did they have straws too?

Peeking around the aisle, the Rabbid saw two of his fellow Rabbids laughing hysterically.

They were not blowing into straws, though. They were watching an old lady open and close a freezer door.

"Oh, chicken wings!" said the lady, holding up a box of ice-cream bars. "I just love chicken wings." She put the box in her cart and shut the freezer door.

The Rabbids stopped laughing.

Luckily (for the Rabbids at least), this particular lady was a little confused, and she soon opened the same door again. This time she picked up a box of ice pops and stared at it closely.

"What was I looking for again?" said the lady. "I can't read a thing without my glasses!"

While the old lady was busy trying
to decide if she wanted the ice pops (or
possibly trying to decide if they were ice
pops) the Rabbids inched closer and closer
to the open freezer.

At that moment the old lady decided that she did want the ice pops (or whatever she thought they were). She threw them in her cart and slammed the freezer door shut with her foot, trapping one of the Rabbids inside!

CHAPTER 2:
RABBID TUNA

The trapped Rabbid shivered because it was, well, freezing inside the freezer, but then he quickly forgot about how cold he was when he realized he was someplace new and exciting!

First the Rabbid had fun smacking his hands on the glass. Then he had fun smacking his head on the glass. Smacking anything with your head doesn't sound like a lot of fun to a person, but it's fun if you're a Rabbid.

Then he had a brilliant idea and decided to put his tongue on the glass. This was exciting because his tongue got stuck! He was having so much fun he didn't notice that his legs were starting to freeze. . . .

The Rabbid's partner, who wasn't in the freezer, put his tongue on his side of the glass. Because his side of the glass wasn't frozen, however, his tongue wouldn't stick. Of course the Rabbid didn't understand that, so he ended up just licking the glass a bunch of times.

These two Rabbids looked like they
were having such a good time that the first
Rabbid we met, the one with the straw,
wanted to join in. But being on two sides of
some glass is really a two-player game
(if it's a game at all), so this Rabbid was
left out.

The Rabbid was walking away sadly when all of a sudden the old lady came back!

"I almost forgot the ice cream!" she exclaimed, opening the freezer door and picking up a box of fish sticks.

The Rabbid saw his chance. He made a run for the open freezer door, and he was almost there when . . .

SMACK! The other Rabbid had beat him into the freezer, and the old lady had closed the door in his face.

The left-out Rabbid sat up, a little stunned from being smacked with the freezer door—and then he noticed that the Rabbid in the freezer had an ice-cream carton stuck on his butt! *Bwa ha ha!*

Having an ice-cream carton stuck to your butt might seem like a problem, but this Rabbid saw it as an opportunity—to dance! He wiggled his bottom, and the ice-cream carton wiggled with him.

The Rabbid outside of the freezer was not happy. He was feeling really left out now and wanted to go in the freezer and dance with a carton attached to his butt too!

Meanwhile, the old lady continued to look for whatever she was looking for when something caught her eye. "Oooooh," she squealed. "What a gorgeous piece of tuna!" She picked up the Rabbid with the carton attached to his butt and carried him off to her cart.

CHAPTER 3:
STORE SURFING

At this point, the first Rabbid in the freezer (you forgot about him, didn't you?) was starting to think that maybe this cold chamber wasn't quite so fun. His ears were stuck to the glass, and his whole bottom half was completely frozen! (And yes, that means his butt was frozen too.)

Meanwhile, the old lady had decided maybe she didn't want the tuna (really the Rabbid) after all.

"This smells like it has gone bad," she complained. And with that, she tossed the Rabbid across the store.

By now the ice-cream carton had melted enough that it became unfrozen from the Rabbid's butt, and the Rabbid landed right on top of it. He went sailing across the floor, screaming in confusion . . . until he realized he could use the carton as a surfboard!

The Rabbid surfed all around the store, doing tricks and having the time of his life. He probably never would have stopped, but something made him stop, and I bet you can guess what it was. . . .

That's right: He was stopped by a giant display of canned vegetables.

The other Rabbids watched the collision happen and thought it looked like fun. They ran toward the freezer and tried to pry open the door with a fork.

The Rabbid who had wanted to get into the freezer so badly before now really, really wanted to get in so he could get his own ice-cream-carton skateboard.

CHAPTER 4:
A NEW TACTIC

Trying his best to look cute and innocent, this left-out Rabbid walked up to a young woman pushing a cart.

"Awww," said the woman, smiling down at the Rabbid.

"Bwa, bwa bwa bwa bwa bwa bwa?" he asked sweetly, pointing at the freezer door.

The woman looked confused. And she didn't open the door.

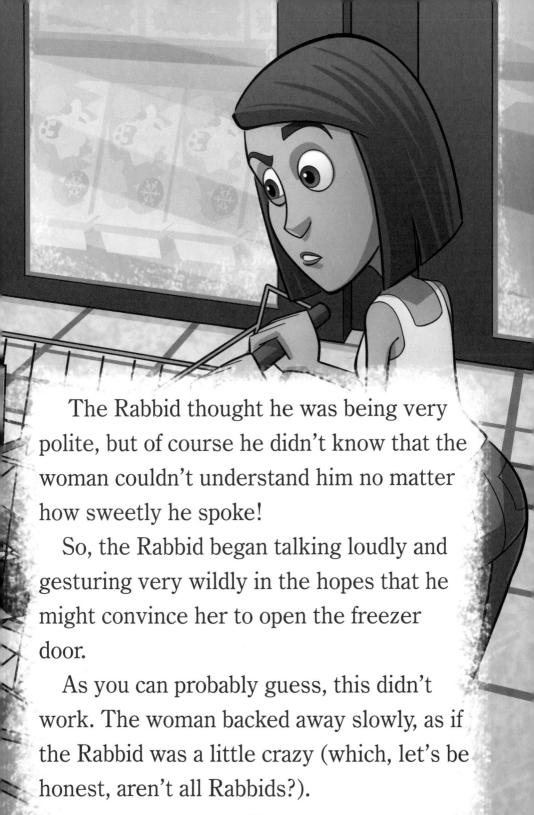

The Rabbid thought he was being very polite, but of course he didn't know that the woman couldn't understand him no matter how sweetly he spoke!

So, the Rabbid began talking loudly and gesturing very wildly in the hopes that he might convince her to open the freezer door.

As you can probably guess, this didn't work. The woman backed away slowly, as if the Rabbid was a little crazy (which, let's be honest, aren't all Rabbids?).

The left-out Rabbid was getting really desperate. When the old lady approached the freezer for what seemed like the seventeenth time, he latched himself onto her leg.

Without her cart to hold onto, the lady quickly lost her balance, but she grabbed onto another customer as she went down. This poor man, the old lady, and the Rabbid twirled around and around until they crashed . . . right into the freezer door the other Rabbids were trying to open.

The door opened and all of the ice-cream cartons came tumbling out, onto the man who was now lying flat on the floor.

"Don't worry, I'm perfectly fine," said the old lady as she walked away.

The three Rabbids who had been trying to open the door quickly snatched frozen boxes. The completely frozen Rabbid, who was still stuck in the freezer, watched as his fellow Rabbids performed a variety of tricks using the boxes. It didn't occur to any of the performing Rabbids to go help their frozen friend.

The left-out Rabbid also watched as the other Rabbids played with the cartons. What fun he could have with a frozen ice-cream carton! He would probably put it on his butt. Or maybe his head. He went to get a carton of his own, but when he looked down . . .

the boxes were completely gone.

CHAPTER 5:
THE LAST STRAW

This was the last straw for the left-out Rabbid. He screamed in frustration. He picked up soda bottles and threw them. He kicked boxes of cereal. Then he screamed some more.

Finally the Rabbid gave up and sat quietly on the ground. He picked up the straw he had loved playing with earlier with and blew into it halfheartedly. A weak *pfft* came out, and the Rabbid threw the straw toward the freezer.

The man had just gotten up, and the straw hit him in the face. The Rabbid hadn't meant to do this, but if he had been in a better mood, he probably would have found it funny. Anyway, the man jumped in fright, spun around, and crashed into the freezer door before running away, whimpering. Then something amazing happened.

The door opened.

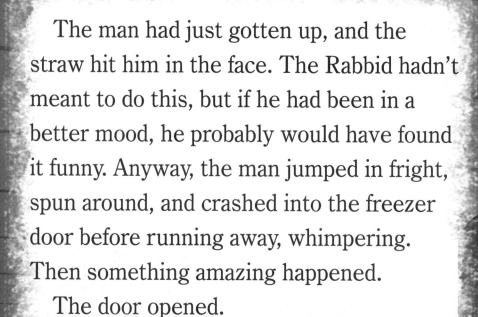

It was just what the poor left-out Rabbid had been waiting for! Well, at least for the last few minutes, since he had realized that freezer doors could open and Rabbids could go inside. He hopped right into the freezer and started dancing around.

He only danced for a moment before he realized that the first Rabbid to enter the freezer was completely frozen and stuck to the freezer door.

He tapped the frozen Rabbid and it slid off the door and onto the floor, still sliding. This gave him another idea. . . .

CHAPTER 6:
THE BIG THAW

While three of the Rabbids were still gliding around on ice-cream cartons, the other Rabbid came speeding by . . . surfing on the frozen Rabbid! This was the best toy of all. The Rabbids had a blast surfing around the store, crashing down as many displays as they could and knocking over lots of carts.

When the Rabbids were finally tired of causing chaos (or playing, as they thought of it), they lay down on what seemed to them like a moving bed.

The cashier picked up a Rabbid attached to a frozen pizza and rang it up. Then he picked up a Rabbid attached to an ice-cream carton and rang it up.

"Goodness!" said the old lady. "I don't remember getting all this."

Just then, the frozen Rabbid, who was starting to thaw, slid out of the cart and onto the floor. He used his unfrozen arm to start to propel himself away from the checkout. Finally, he was getting a chance to have some fun!

"Hey, my lima beans!" cried the old lady. "They're getting away!"